"Are you an expert on evil, Rosamund?"

When she turned back to him her eyes were a bit wild—large and round, lost in that pretty face. They startled him. So did her answer. "Aye. Of a sort. I am."

He blinked, trying to absorb it. Trying to think what it meant. In the end, he only held out his hand. "Come. Let us go back to the hall."

She was so artless, so utterly transparent. She hesitated. "I...I thought I might roam a bit. Get to know the castle."

"What a poor liar you are."

Her head whipped around. She was all fire again. "What an insulting man you are! What reason have you to question me?"

What reason had he? Only that something deep down in his gut seemed connected to this woman. Only that his soul spoke to him of her, and it told him disturbing things....

Dear Reader,

Much of the beauty of romance novels is that most are written by women for women, and feature strong and passionate heroines. We have some stellar authors this month who bring to life those intrepid women we love as they engage in relationships with the men we also love!

In fact, rising talent Jacqueline Navin could be one of our heroines. This mother of three has written six books since her publishing debut in 1998. Her latest, *The Viking's Heart,* is a lively yet emotional sequel to her first book, *The Maiden and the Warrior.* Here, noblewoman Rosamund Clavier awaits escort to the dreaded marriage her abusive father has arranged for her. Imagine Rosamund's dilemma when she discovers that her Viking escort is her true match—yet duty and honor still bind her to another....

Award-winning author Gayle Wilson returns with *My Lady's Dare,* a sensational Regency-set romance about a woman who would sacrifice all for the life of a family member. Luckily the Earl of Dare comes to *her* rescue! In *Bandera's Bride,* Mary McBride gives her Southern belle heroine some serious chutzpah when, pregnant and alone, she travels to Texas to propose marriage to her pen pal of six years, a half-breed who's been signing his partner's name...!

And don't miss Susan Amarillas's new Western, *Molly's Hero,* a story of forbidden love between a female rancher and the handsome railroad builder who needs her land.

Enjoy! And come back again next month for four more choices of the best in historical romance.

Sincerely,

Tracy Farrell,
Senior Editor